To Ken — PB
For Freya and Freddie — AG

Thank you to Dr. David Ng for fact-checking Professor Goose's fact-checking. — PB

Text copyright © 2022 by Contextx Inc.
Illustrations copyright © 2022 by Alex G. Griffiths

Tundra Books, an imprint of Penguin Random House Canada Young Readers, a division of Penguin Random House of Canada Limited

Library and Archives Canada Cataloguing in Publication

Title: Professor Goose debunks Goldilocks and the three bears / Paulette Bourgeois ; [illustrated by] Alex G. Griffiths.
Other titles: Based on (expression): Goldilocks and the three bears. English.
Names: Bourgeois, Paulette, author. | Griffiths, Alex G, illustrator.
Identifiers: Canadiana (print) 20210255552 | Canadiana (ebook) 20210255609 | ISBN 9780735267305 (hardcover) | ISBN 9780735267312 (EPUB)
Classification: LCC PS8553.O85477 P76 2022 | DDC jC813/.54—dc23

Published simultaneously in the United States of America by Tundra Books of Northern New York,
an imprint of Penguin Random House Canada Young Readers, a division of Penguin Random House of Canada Limited

Library of Congress Control Number: 2021942063

Acquired by Tara Walker
Edited by Elizabeth Kribs with Margot Blankier
Designed by John Martz and Sophie Paas-Lang
The illustrations in this book were created with pen and ink, and colored with mixed media and digitally.
The text was set in Colby and LTC Cloister Oldstyle.

Printed in China

www.penguinrandomhouse.ca

1 2 3 4 5   26 25 24 23 22

Penguin
Random House
TUNDRA BOOKS

Professor Goose Debunks
GOLDILOCKS and the THREE BEARS

WRITTEN BY *Paulette Bourgeois*

ILLUSTRATED BY *Alex G. Griffiths*

tundra

ONCE UPON A TIME, there was a papa bear, a mama bear and a baby bear who lived in a cottage by the woods. They made porridge for breakfast, but it was too hot to eat, so they went for a walk while it cooled.

Really?

Bears don't live like us. They have their own **natural habitat**.

Bears don't live in cottages with curtains on the windows. They live in dens.

Bears don't eat porridge. Well, maybe if there were honey and nuts and berries on top.

Now I'm hungry as a bear.

HA!

Professor Goose's Fact Check

Biologists study life and living things. They tell us that, in their **natural habitat**, some bears make dens under the roots of trees, others dig into hills or find cozy caves and some, like polar bears, make dens in snow. Bears usually eat what they find in their habitats. Some of them like human garbage, but it's unhealthy for them. Pandas are the pickiest eaters: most of them eat only bamboo.

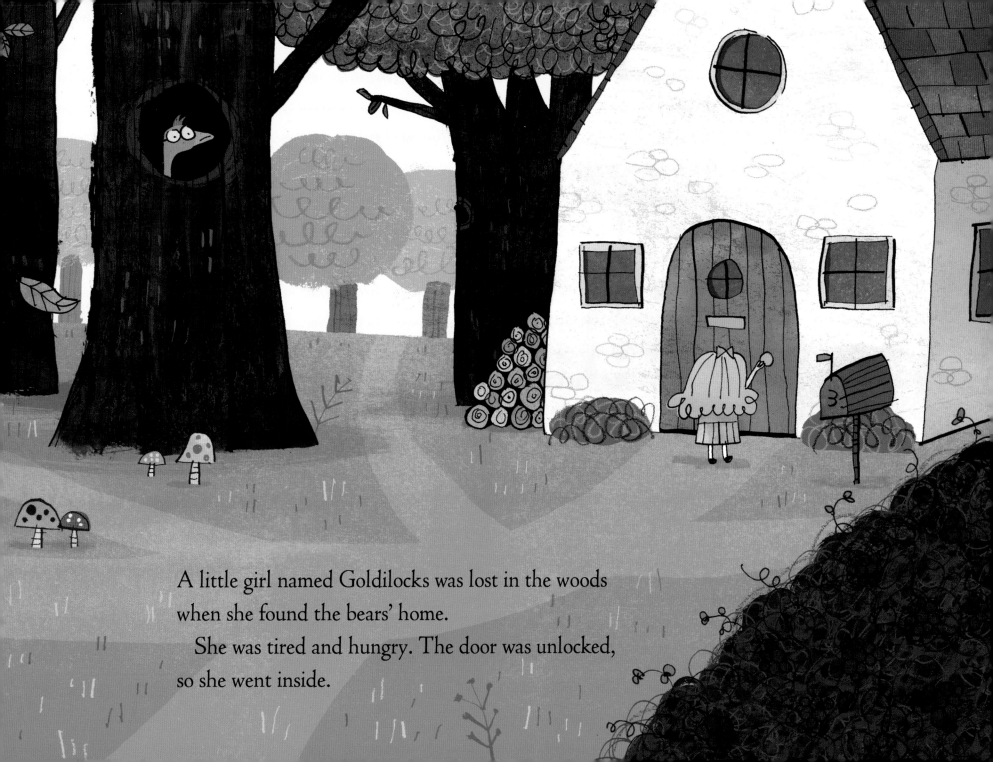

A little girl named Goldilocks was lost in the woods
when she found the bears' home.

She was tired and hungry. The door was unlocked,
so she went inside.

Professor Goose's Fact Check

Satellites that float high above the earth send out radio signals that are received by your phone, which will pinpoint where you are and where you're going — this is called **GPS** or Global Positioning System.

Before the Bear family went on their walk, Papa Bear had put a big scoop of hot porridge into his big bowl. He put a medium-sized scoop into Mama Bear's medium-sized bowl. And he put a teensy-weensy scoop into Baby Bear's teensy-weensy bowl.

Goldilocks was ravenous.

She tasted the porridge in the big bowl.
"Too hot!" she said.

She tasted the porridge
in the medium-sized bowl.
"Too cold!" she said.

Then Goldilocks tasted the porridge in the
teensy-weensy bowl.
"Just right!" she said. And she gobbled it all up.

Professor Goose's Fact Check

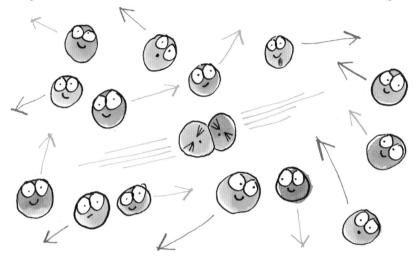

Thermodynamics is a big word for a BIG idea in science. Its laws explain how heat and energy move through the universe. Porridge, like almost everything else, is made up of many particles that are too small to see with the naked eye. As the porridge cooked, the particles moved faster and faster, increasing thermal energy. Thermodynamics tells us that hot porridge cools down as its thermal energy moves toward the cooler air around it. With more particles in the big bowl, there was more thermal energy, so it took longer to cool. If Goldilocks had waited, eventually the porridge in the big, the medium-sized and the teensy-weensy bowls would all have become the same temperature as the air.

Goldilocks was very tired and
needed to sit down.

She sat in Papa Bear's chair.
"Too hard," she said.

Next she sat in Mama
Bear's chair. "Too soft,"
she said.

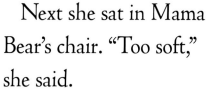

And then she sat in Baby Bear's chair.
"Just right," she said.

CRACK! The chair broke.
WHAM! Goldilocks fell to the ground.

OUCH! **Downward forces** can be a pain in the rump!

And now poor Baby Bear is without a chair because Goldilocks didn't know how to fix it! If only she'd taken my class, HOW TO ENGINEER A CHAIR FOR A BEAR.

You can make almost anything from cardboard. Except maybe a toothbrush.

Goldilocks broke the chair because she exerted a **downward force** that was greater than the chair's **upward force**. In other words, she sat down on a chair that was too small and too flimsy to support her weight.

Goldilocks yawned.

Upstairs she discovered three beds.

She tried Papa Bear's bed. "Too hard!" she said.

She tried Mama Bear's bed.
"Too soft!" she said.

And then she tried Baby Bear's bed.
"Just right!" she said.
And Goldilocks fell fast asleep.

YAWN! I feel sleepy, too. Sometimes I wish geese could **hibernate**.

Every animal — bears and little children and professors — needs sleep.

Sleep helps our brains sort out what we've learned and helps us grow healthy bodies.

We dream during the deepest part of sleep.

I dream of winning the Nobel Prize for revealing the faulty science in fairy tales!

Professor Goose's Fact Check

Hibernation is a type of long, very deep sleep. But did you know that bears don't actually hibernate? Some animals like bats have a true hibernation where their heartbeats become very slow and they don't wake up when disturbed. Some kinds of bears fall into a different type of sleep called **torpor** in winter. They can sleep for more than a hundred days without eating, drinking or going to the bathroom, but they can wake easily from torpor if hurt or threatened. Mama bears even have babies and then fall asleep again! P.S. The babies sleep happily until spring, too!

When the three bears came home, they were surprised to find that things were not as they left them.

"Somebody ate our porridge!" said Papa Bear.

"Somebody sat in our chairs!" said Mama Bear.

"Somebody BROKE my chair!" said Baby Bear. "But who?"

FABULOUS! Baby Bear might be a budding scientist. I think she's about to use the **scientific method** to solve the mystery.

The **scientific method** is a set of steps that scientists and many others use to test their ideas. It starts with an OBSERVATION and a QUESTION. To answer that question, they make a HYPOTHESIS, which is a good guess about what causes something to happen. They test their hypothesis and collect and record information called data. Then they come to a CONCLUSION and share what they have learned with others.

Baby Bear observed the following:

Some porridge was missing from her parents' bowls, and her bowl was empty.

There was a long, curly blond hair in the empty bowl.

Papa's and Mama's chairs had been moved, and hers was completely destroyed.

And a trail of muddy footprints went up the stairs to the bedroom.

She said, "I hypothesize that we have a hungry blond human who came in from the woods who is bigger and heavier than me but not as big as either of you."

"Is it still here?" asked Mama Bear.

"I predict that it is somewhere in the house. Probably upstairs," said Baby Bear, pointing to the muddy footprints.

They crept into the bedroom.
    "There it is!" cried Baby Bear.

Goldilocks woke with a start. She took one look at the bears, then leapt out of bed and escaped through the window.

"Don't go!" cried Baby Bear, but Goldilocks was already far away.

YIKES! Good thing she landed in that bush. I sure hope it wasn't poison ivy! Goldilocks must have been really scared, which triggered a typical **fight or flight response**.

When we are frightened, our brains try to protect us with a **fight or flight response**. If we sense danger — like what happens when we face a scary animal — our brain sends a message to our muscles to tense up so we can fight off the danger or take flight and escape.

That's where the story usually ends, but based on my observations of the Bear family, I propose another conclusion . . .

PLEASE Knock Before Enter

Papa Bear rubbed his growling tummy and said, "If that little girl ever comes back, she had better bring some berries."

Mama Bear made a sign for the front door.

And Baby Bear designed and built herself a brand-new chair.

Turn the page to find out how YOU can engineer a chair for a bear!

HOW TO ENGINEER A CHAIR FOR A BEAR
Calling all budding engineers — you can make a chair!

You'll need:

- 3 square pieces of cardboard, about 9 in. (24 cm) on each side (ask an adult to help you cut out the pieces)
- 4 empty toilet paper rolls (make sure you've already used up all the toilet paper on them, HA!)
- 1 cardboard egg carton

- some scrap paper or newsprint
- craft glue
- tape (wide tape like duct tape or masking tape works best)
- 2 craft or Popsicle sticks, about 8 in. (20 cm) long
- a sharp knife or scissors — ask for an adult's help when using!

Step 1: Make the seat of the chair

To make a sturdy seat, we'll make what I like to call a seat sandwich! Take a sheet of scrap paper and roll it into a tight tube like a straw, then tape it at both ends so it stays rolled up. Make enough straws to cover 1 square of cardboard. This is the filling to the sandwich!

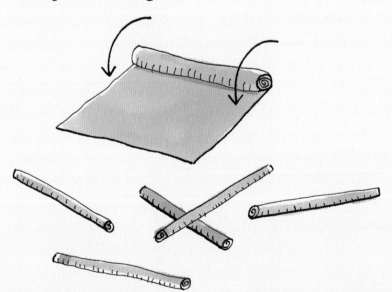

Next, glue the straws to 1 side of a cardboard square, then take a second square of cardboard and glue it on top to complete the seat sandwich. (Warning: it tastes terrible — do not eat!) Trim any bits of straw that are sticking out of the sandwich.

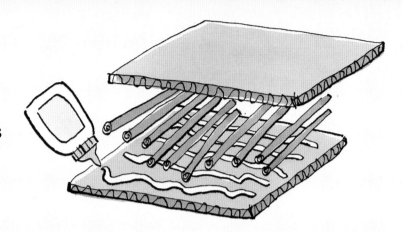

Step 2: Build the legs

For the legs, we'll use the toilet paper rolls, the egg carton and tape. The toilet paper rolls will be the legs, but they need to be reinforced before we can stick them on the chair.

Separate the egg carton into at least 8 cups. (Use your hands to tear it or ask for an adult's help with scissors.) Now, squish 1 cup into each end of the toilet paper rolls, then seal it in place with tape.

Glue the end of 1 toilet paper roll to each corner of the seat sandwich. You've got a fine stool now, but keep going if you want to make a chair with a back!

Step 3: Build the back

To make the back of the chair, we'll use our remaining piece of cardboard, our craft sticks, glue, a sharp knife or scissors — and an adult! The craft sticks will go into the seat and help the back of the chair stand up.

Pick a side of the seat. With an adult's help, use the knife or scissors to cut 2 horizontal slits the same width as the craft sticks into the top and filling of the seat sandwich. Gently slide the craft sticks into the slits until they hit the bottom of the seat sandwich.

Now tip the chair over so the craft sticks are flat on your work surface. Apply some glue to the craft sticks, then put your remaining piece of cardboard on the glue.

Once the glue dries . . .

Congratulations! You've engineered a chair. Now you're ready to invite a bear to lunch. But don't give her porridge!

**Thanks to my budding engineers for their chair designs:
Marlowe, Rowan, Forrester and Leo.**